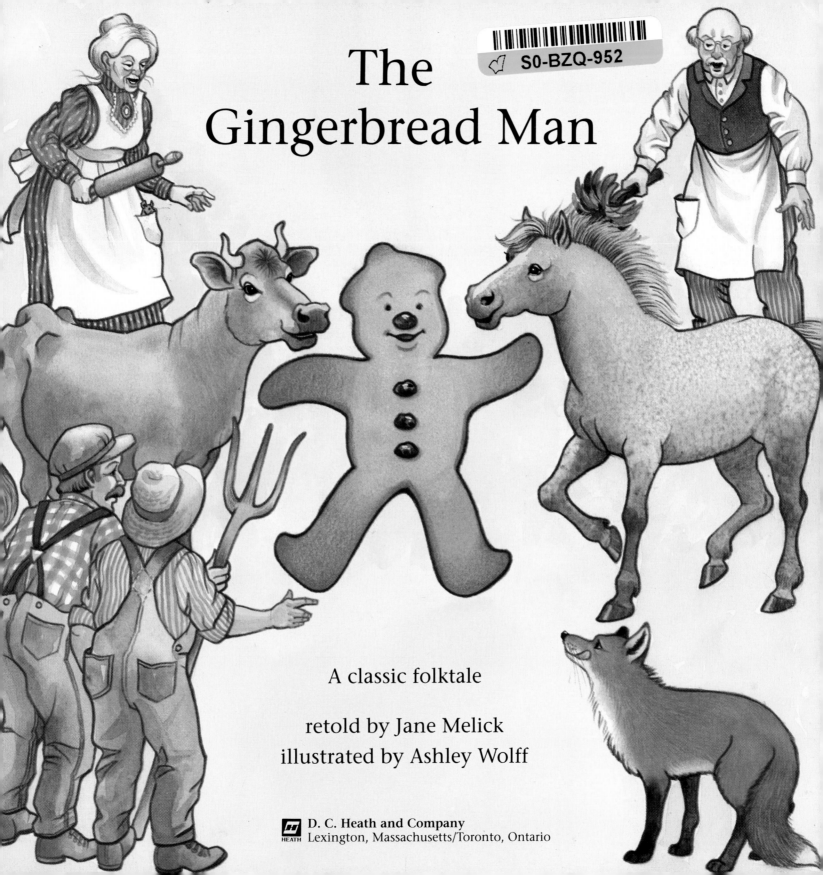

The Gingerbread Man

A classic folktale

retold by Jane Melick

illustrated by Ashley Wolff

D. C. Heath and Company
Lexington, Massachusetts/Toronto, Ontario

Gingerbread Men
¼ cup butter
½ cup sugar
½ cup molasses
3½ cups flour
1 teaspoon baking soda
¼ teaspoon cloves
2 teaspoons ginger
½ teaspoon cinnamon
½ teaspoon salt

Once upon a time a little old woman and a little old man lived in a little old house. They lived all alone. One day, the little old woman was making gingerbread.

4

"Mix and bake, mix and bake.
A little Gingerbread Man I make.
With a hat on his head
And mouth, eyes, and nose.
I'll put him on a pan,
Then into the oven he goes."

5

The little old woman put the little Gingerbread Man into the oven. Then she went to help the little old man who had started to clean the house. They forgot all about the little Gingerbread Man.

"Sniff, sniff, what's that I smell? Mercy! It's gingerbread burning. I know that smell well!"

So the little old woman and the little old man
ran to the oven and opened the door.
Out jumped the Gingerbread Man. He ran
across the kitchen and out the door as fast as his
little gingerbread legs would carry him. The little
old man and the little old woman ran after him.

"Stop! Stop,
Little Gingerbread Man!
You really should cool
On the gingerbread pan."

But the Gingerbread Man kept on running and laughing. He called out:

"Run! Run! Run!
As fast as you can.
You can't catch me,
I'm the Gingerbread Man!
I am! I am!"

And they couldn't catch him.

So the Gingerbread Man ran on and on.
Soon he came to a cow. The cow sniffed
the Gingerbread Man.

"Gingerbread Man, you smell so sweet,
And gingerbread is very good to eat."

But the little Gingerbread Man laughed
and said:

"I've run away from a little old woman,
I've run away from a little old man,
And I can run away from you, I can, I can!"

13

The cow ran after him. But the Gingerbread Man
kept on running and laughing. He called out:

"Run! Run! Run!
As fast as you can.
You can't catch me,
I'm the Gingerbread Man!
I am! I am!"

And the cow couldn't catch him.

So the Gingerbread Man ran on and on.
Soon he came to a horse. The horse sniffed
the Gingerbread Man.

"Gingerbread Man, you smell so sweet,
And gingerbread is very good to eat."

But the little Gingerbread Man laughed
and said:

"I've run away from a little old woman,
I've run away from a little old man,
I've run away from a cow,
And I can run away from you, I can, I can!"

17

The horse ran after him. But the Gingerbread Man kept on running and laughing. He called out:

"Run! Run! Run!
As fast as you can.
You can't catch me,
I'm the Gingerbread Man!
I am! I am!"

And the horse couldn't catch him.

So the Gingerbread Man
ran on and on.
Soon he came to some
farmers working in a barn.
The farmers sniffed
the Gingerbread Man.

"Gingerbread Man,
you smell so sweet,
And gingerbread
is very good to eat."

But the little Gingerbread Man laughed
and said:

"I've run away from a little old woman,
I've run away from a little old man,
I've run away from a cow,
I've run away from a horse,
And I can run away from you, I can, I can!"

The farmers ran after him. But
the Gingerbread Man kept on
running and laughing. He called out:

"Run! Run! Run!
As fast as you can.
You can't catch me,
I'm the Gingerbread Man!
I am! I am!"

And the farmers couldn't catch him.

23

By this time the little Gingerbread Man was very proud of himself. He strutted. He danced. He thought no one on earth could catch him!

Pretty soon he saw a fox coming across a field.
The fox looked at him and began to run.
The Gingerbread Man ran faster and shouted
out:

"I've run away from a little old woman,
I've run away from a little old man,
I've run away from a cow,
I've run away from a horse,
I've run away from a barn full of farmers,
And I can run away from you, I can, I can!"

But the fox said politely:

"Gingerbread Man,
Don't you worry.
I'm not chasing you,
I'm just in a hurry."

Soon the little Gingerbread Man came to a river.
The cow, the horse, and the farmers were still
chasing him. He could not jump into the water
because he would fall apart if he got wet.
He had to get to the other side!

"Jump on my tail,
I will take you across.
We'll swim the deep river,"
Said the sly old fox.

The Gingerbread Man hopped onto the fox's tail.

"Now get on my back
So you don't fall in.
The water is deep,"
The fox said with a grin.

The Gingerbread Man
hopped onto the fox's back.

30

When they were near the other side of the river, the fox cried out:

"The water grows deeper,
Jump up on my nose.
You must not get wet,
Not even your toes."

So the Gingerbread Man jumped up on the fox's nose.

Just then the fox sprang ashore and threw back his head.

Snip, snap, snip, snap,
Is how the story goes.
The Gingerbread Man was gone
Clear down to his toes!